TWO SIDES of the COIN

Stories by
Geraldine McCaughrean and Jan Mark

Illustrations by Adam Stower,
David Roberts and Rosalind Hudson

Contents

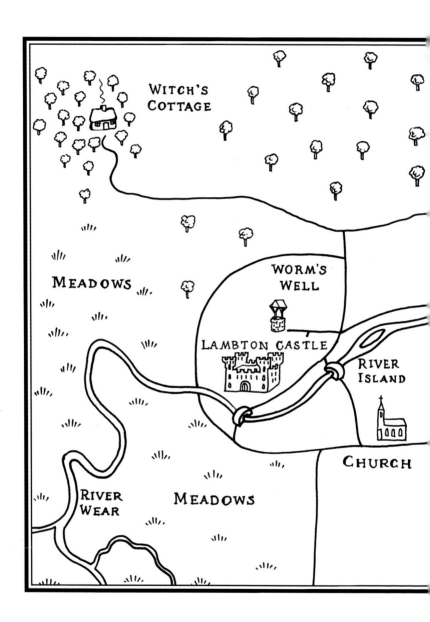

WITCH'S COTTAGE

WORM'S WELL

MEADOWS

LAMBTON CASTLE

RIVER ISLAND

CHURCH

RIVER WEAR

MEADOWS

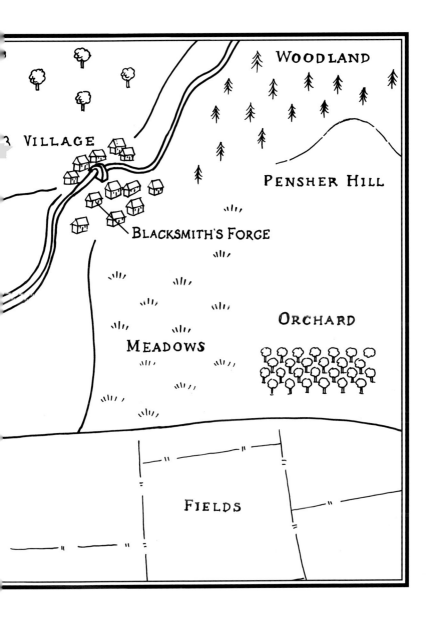

WOODLAND

R VILLAGE

PENSHER HILL

BLACKSMITH'S FORGE

ORCHARD

MEADOWS

FIELDS

The Lambton Worm

Retold by Geraldine McCaughrean

Long ago, when wickedness lurked round every dark corner, a boy went fishing. He should not have gone. It was Sunday, and he should have been in church. But John Lambton was not the best of boys – not much better, in fact, than you. So all day long, instead of sitting in church, he sat by the river, trying to glimpse the gleaming

grey trout beneath the glittering surface.

But all he caught was a worm.

It was tiny – no good for eating, no good for boasting about. In fact, the worm was good for nothing but putting down the back of his sister's dress ... or back on the hook. So John put the worm on his hook and tossed it back into the river. But it seemed as if that worm, for all its smallness, frightened away every fish in the river. Suddenly the swim was empty of everything but water and weed and worm. Across the fields, the church bells tolled for evening service, but John Lambton did not listen.

John reeled in his worm and strolled idly back home, tossing the little wriggler high in the air off the palm of his hand and catching it again. As he passed the well in the rear courtyard, he tossed the worm away. Perhaps it would come up in a bucket of water and give the cook a scare, or be found swimming in the soup when his sister ate her supper. No, John Lambton was not the best of boys: certainly, no better than you.

But the worm did not surface either in the kitchen or at supper. Soon it was forgotten. And do you know what? As John grew older, he grew into a much better, braver, bolder breed of man – the pride of his mother and a credit to his father. Even his sister liked him when he was full-grown. John's father was Lord of Lambton, so he could have chosen to live in comfort, doing nothing but fishing all day or hunting with his greyhounds. Instead, John became a knight – a Crusader – and travelled far afield – to Byzantium, Manzikert and Jerusalem. And all the while he travelled, he grew in fame and in bravery.

And all the while, down in the well, the worm was growing, too.

Like a tadpole, it sprouted legs, but this was no tadpole. Like a newt its tail grew longer, but this was no newt. Like a snake it put on scales, but this was no snake. Down in the deep darkness of the well, it grew and grew and grew. Unlike John Lambton, it grew in wickedness, too.

Terrible things began to happen. Shepherds found their sheep lying dead in the field. Pigs and calves went missing. Horses and cows strayed out of sight, overnight and were never seen again. Lord Lambton thought, 'Outlaws or rustlers.' His peasants thought, 'The Devil!'

Fences were wrenched from the ground. The vines were trampled flat. Lord Lambton thought, 'High winds?' His peasants thought, 'The Devil!'

The few cows left would not give milk; there was nothing to drink but water, and the water tasted vile. The crops lay flat as a woven mat. The orchards were stripped of fruit. Lord Lambton thought, 'I wish my son was home.' His peasants thought, 'So do we.'

In order to find out the cause of all his troubles, Lord Lambton posted men to keep watch all night. 'Report to me in the morning and tell me what you saw,' he said. But he did not have to wait till morning. Their screaming woke him at four. They hammered at the door to come in. Their hair was grey with terror and their faces grey with fright.

'It came out of the well, master! It hauled itself out of the well!'

'A dragonish thing it was, sir, with spines and claws and a terrible mouthful of teeth!'

'It will kill us all in our beds, squire! It will eat us all like chickens!' and they packed up their carts with babies and wives and they left the county that day.

So Lord Lambton offered a reward to whatever brave soul would fight the Worm and kill it. Some poured oil down the well and lit it. Some threw down rocks and spears. Some tried poisoned meat and hunting traps. But the Worm in the well could eat fire – and belch it, too. The Worm could eat poison and thrive on it. The Worm could crush rocks and mantraps to dust between its fearful teeth.

Some even tried fighting the Worm face to face, but they all died trying. For you could hack and chop at its hide and still it would not die. Indeed, the Worm would simply slither across its own gory shreds of flesh and absorb them again, like a river absorbing a bucket of water. What is more, the Worm resented these feeble, fruitless attacks, and in its anger it always took some terrible revenge. It ripped the roofs from cottages, scattered the haystacks or uprooted the trees in an acre of woodland.

So instead of fighting it, Lord Lambton tried to keep the beast at bay with offerings of food. He poured milk into the well and left goats or sheep tethered beside it. As a result, the villagers went hungry and the Worm did not. It grew fatter and longer, fitter and stronger. Now, at night, when it pulled itself out of the well and dragged its scaly belly over the empty fields, it was so immense that it could curl itself three times round nearby Pensher Hill. Round and round it wound itself, like a ship's rope around a capstan. Then it lay looking at the moon, as though it might rear up soon and take a bite.

The people could hear it breathing and growling and grinding its teeth and they trembled in their beds. 'This is the work of the Devil,' they said, and Lord Lambton said, 'They are not wrong.'

When word went out about the Worm in the well, no one came to Lambton Castle any more, and no one left there. Even during the day, people in the neighbourhood were too afraid to venture out of doors.

So when John Lambton came riding home from the Crusades, he rode through a landscape empty of people, empty of animals, empty of crops. Even the trees lay flat along the ground, like dead men. The cottages without their roofs looked like pigless sties. John's heart shrank inside him with dread. Whatever had happened to his father's estates while he was away?

Lord Lambton was so delighted to see his son home safe that he gave orders for a great feast, and invited everyone he knew and several people he had never even heard of! The turrets were strung with pennants. The walls were hung with swags of scarlet cloth. At sunny noon (the safest time of day) musicians and acrobats, jugglers and actors made a wild dash for Castle Lambton and got ready to put on a jolly show.

John Lambton was not fooled. He could see the white hairs on their heads, the trembling of their hands, the nervous stammer in their voices. He could see that worry had made his father old and creased the beauty of his mother's face.

'What has happened here while I've

been gone? Were you attacked? Is the country at war? What brought down the trees over yonder and flattened all the crops?'

A dreadful silence fell over the room. The jugglers came to a fumbling finish. The musicians broke off. Everyone at table suddenly lost their appetite and stopped eating. Heads drooped in misery as Lord Lambton told his son the terrible news about the monster in the well.

For John, it was as if all the candles in the room flickered and went out. All at once he knew – without a shadow of a doubt – how his Sunday fishing trip had caused their misery. His careless prank, his silly boyhood joke had brought disaster to family and friends alike. Slowly, awkwardly, he explained how he had caught the worm in the River Wear and tossed it into the well.

'It was my doing, and I must undo it,' he said at last. 'I must fight the Worm and kill it. Then life can go back to the way it was! ... At least I have to try.'

He was no coward. In the Holy Land he had fought the Saracens and the Turks. He had sweated in the desert and frozen in alpine snow, but he had no experience of fighting dragons – especially those that could wind themselves five times around the church.

A kind of sigh went round the room. Faces relaxed; mouths twitched into half-smiles. Their shining hero, back from the Lands of God, was going to fight the Worm. Maybe, despite everything, all might be well after all.

For three weeks John Lambton racked his brains for ideas. Every plan he put to his father had already been tried.

'What if I poured oil into the well and set it alight?'

'The beast cannot be burned.'

'What if I wait till it's sleeping and cut out its heart?'

'It would only grow another.'

'What if I were to drop rocks down the well?'

'It would grind them to dust in its mouth.'

In the end, John knew that he needed the help of Magic – not to fight the Worm (because he was no magician), but to find the well-worm's weakness.

So he went in secret to visit a witch – a

woman whose dreams were older and more magic than those of other women. He did not tell his mother, because she would have forbidden it. He did not tell his father, because he would rather have lived with the Worm than dabble in magic.

'You have come about the Worm,' said the witch, as she opened her cottage door.

'I have come about the Worm,' said John, 'and how to kill it. Even if its body is cut in two, it can join the two halves. I have fought against camels and tigers, eagles and Saracens, but never against a foe who could heal itself over and over again.'

'Worms can do that,' said the old woman, nodding.

'Cut them in two
And they'll renew.
But cut them in twelve or twenty-five,
And even a demon can't keep alive!
He-he-he!'

She plucked a piece of coal from the fire and scrawled on the wall a great dark life-size figure of a man waist deep in wriggles of coaly water. He was as spiny as a porcupine. His arms and legs and body and head were a rash of jagged zigzags and exclamation marks. It made John shiver even to look at it.

'What kind of monster is that? Not the Worm, I know!'

'Nay, lad. That's *you!*' said the witch with another bleat of laughter. 'If you want to kill the Worm, you must cover your armour in razors and spikes and take your stand in the river. When the Worm comes, and winds round and round you like Pensher Hill, it will cut itself in pieces ...'

'But then it will ...'

'The river will carry the pieces away too fast for the Worm to mend, and when it is dead, there you shall be, like Old Saint George himself!'

John did not like to hear the name of a saint spoken by a witch, but he knew that she was right. He knew he had found the way to kill the Worm – if only he had the courage to do it, and if only he did not drown.

'What do I owe you for your advice?' he asked, taking out his purse.

'The advice is free, John Lambton,' said the witch, 'but all magic carries a price. The price of this magic is death.'

'You mean I shall die?' said John, his voice breaking in his throat. Well, so be it. It could not be helped. His foolishness had brought the Worm to Lambton. He deserved to die in its jaws.

'Nay, nay, lad! I mean that if you live, you must kill the first living creature you see when you come out of the river. For if you do not, nine generations of Lambtons will die unpeaceful deaths, far from their feather beds.' And she spat into the fire, so that the shadows leaped and the coal-black, cartoon figure on the wall seemed to dance an ugly dance.

It sounded like a terrible price to have to pay. But at once, John Lambton put one part of his clever brain to work on a plan to overcome this unfortunate drawback. There are ways and ways of paying such a debt. He thanked the witch for her advice and immediately went to the forge to order a suit of armour.

To his father he said, 'I am going to the river now, to fight the Worm. When the fight is won, I shall sound my hunting horn and you must set loose my greyhounds from the kennel in the yard. Come if you must, to see what's left of the monster, but be sure and let the dogs run on ahead. It is important, Father. Don't forget!'

'Of course not. Of course,' said his father.

When John put on the armour he looked like the spiky fruit of a horse-chestnut tree: the conker inside a casing of wicked spines. No one could clasp him in their arms to wish him farewell, for he was all over razors and blades, saw-tooth scythes and wire barbs. The blacksmith had done a fine job of work.

In the centre of the River Wear John took his stand, just as the witch had told him to do. An island the shape of an eye lay so low in the water that now and then it blinked as the water washed over it. The waves washed over John's feet and chilled him to the marrow. But the fear within chilled him even worse.

The Worm came, of course. It came out that night to coil itself around Pensher Hill and to jab its forked tongue at the moon. It came to eat its nightly meal and to drink from the racing river. And down at the river it found an old acquaintance – someone it remembered very dimly, as a man remembers a childhood dream.

John recognised the Worm too; at least he recognised the v-shaped scar in its neck where the hook had snagged it so many years before. John drew out his broadsword.

Perhaps revenge stirred in the Worm's spongy brain. Maybe it was still just hungry. It slithered into the river and wound itself round and round the island. John slapped its snout with the flat of his blade. 'Come and get me, Earthworm!'

The Worm tightened its coils. Round and round it wound itself around John's legs, his body, and his head. Feeling pain, it squeezed tighter, to destroy the cause of the pain. The harder it clung, the more the blades and spikes cut into its scaly hide. The monster's brain was small and dark – like a wormy compost heap – and so it did not grasp the danger. Instead, it grasped John Lambton tighter and tighter, and piece by part it was sliced through to its boneless spine.

'Squeeze tighter, Worm!' gasped John. 'You have not killed me yet!'

As each part and piece fell into the river, it was swept away by the current, tumbled downstream, washed away towards the waiting sea. The monster had no time to heal itself, to knit together again. Instead it shrank, by bits and bobs, to the thickness of a shark, an arm, a chain, a wire ...

And then it was gone.

Green with the blood of the Worm, John Lambton waded ashore, exhausted. The Worm had all but squeezed the breath out of him, and he had to wait a while until his lungs refilled with delicious air. Delightedly, he cast aside his spiked helmet, his razory armour, his barbed boots. Then he put his hunting horn to his lips and blew.

Now all he had to do, to keep his bargain with the Magic, was to take the life of the first creature he met. He would be sad to lose one of his hunting greyhounds, but then John accepted that he deserved some sadness for the misery he had brought on Lambton.

Back at Castle Lambton, up on the castle walls, Lord Lambton heard the noise of the fight. He heard the monster roar. He heard it shriek. He heard it whistle and scream and whimper. Then there was silence and – whole minutes later! – the piercing silver note of a hunting horn.

'He has done it! The boy has done it! Quick! I must greet him! I must thank him! I must congratulate him! Oh, joy of joys! My boy has fought the Worm and lived!'

John took his bow from among the long grass of the riverbank and laid an arrow to its string. It was important he did not miss ...

'... *you must kill the first living creature you see when you come out of the river. For if you do not, nine generations of Lambtons will die unpeaceful deaths, far from their feather beds ...*'

John Lambton stretched his bowstring to his cheek and took careful aim ...

But who should emerge from the morning mist but his own father – running, calling, laughing.

John Lambton felt the bowstring cut into the crook of his fingers. He felt the

arrow fletches kiss his cheek. Then he let go of his arrow ... straight into the ground.

When his father reached him, John was saying, 'I could not do it, Father. I'm sorry.' Over and over again he said it: 'I am so, so very sorry! I could not do it! I could not! I could not pay the price!'

So Castle Lambton was finally free of its terrible Worm. The people danced in the lanes, the lambs pranced in the field, and the meadows grew green again.

But there was no happy ending to the tale of the Worm, because John Lambton had not paid his debt to Magic. From that day on a curse hung over the castle towers, as black as an aching bruise. John's father and John himself died far from home, during the wars with France. John's son and grandson, too; his son and grandson after, died far from the River Wear, far from their wives and children, far from the quiet old age each had promised himself.

For a hundred years war, like a vile worm, wound itself round and around Europe. And in every generation – nine generations in all – a Lambton Lord died an unlucky, early death far from his feather bed.

Each one (or so they say) died cursing the Lambton Worm.

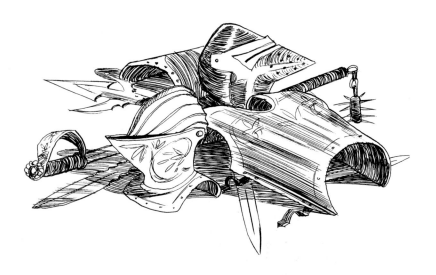

The Grimsditch Worm

by Jan Mark

Lord Grimsditch was a millionaire. He had
begun life as Fred Blackett with one GCSE
in a subject he never talked about, and a
mechanical digger, a second-hand JCB. He
started digging, then he started building.
Anything that could be built, Fred built it:
housing estates, factories, shopping centres,
airports. All over the country his cranes
stood on one leg above cities, with the
name BLACKETT picked out in lights. At
Christmas he erected little fir trees on
them.

When he had made his millions a grateful Government made him a peer of the realm. He chose the title of Baron Grimsditch after the village where he was born, Grimsditch-on-Slype, County Durham.

There was a legend attached to this ditch. Local people said that before the Romans came to Britain the Devil himself had lain down for a nap beside the River Slype, and when he got up again his sinful sulphurous body had burned a great long dent in the landscape, three miles from end to end. The old name for the Devil was Grim, and that great long dent was his ditch, Grimsditch. But the Devil did not have much to do in those days; in the morning he just got up and walked away. Something much worse has been sleeping in the ditch since then.

Lord Grimsditch built a large but tasteful manor house on a hill overlooking Grimsditch-on-Slype and decided to retire there. The locals were not too delighted, but although it had thirty bedrooms and a helipad on the roof it was quite discreet compared to some of the things the old man had built, and he had brought work to the village. Anyway, he was a local man himself and people quite liked him. This was more than could be said of his son and heir who was named United, after Lord Grimsditch's favourite football team.

Before he retired he took United to the top of the company offices in Darlington and pointed out of the window.

'One day,' he said, 'all this will be yours.'

'What, Darlington?' United said, looking all round.

'No, you idiot,' his father said, 'the company. You will inherit my empire, and the title. When I go you will become the second Baron Grimsditch. And let me tell you, son, you've had it soft up till now; it's time you learned to get your hands dirty and do some real work.' He gave him a new JCB to practise with.

Lord Grimsditch drove over to Grimsditch-on-Slype in his Rolls and United followed in the JCB, causing a nine-mile tailback on the A67.

It was on the news that evening: *Grimsditch Heir causes nine-mile tailback on A67*. No one was surprised. The Grimsditch Heir was regularly in the news, crashing cars, trashing hotel rooms and generally making a nuisance of himself.

While Lord Grimsditch settled into Slype Manor young United went out to play with the JCB. He sank a few trenches, for starters, dug up the High Street, took the corner off the Methodist Church and began a small open-cast mine on the southern slope of the Grimsditch itself. The water table in those parts is high. The Heir soon hit liquid.

By this time several people from the village, on their way to Slype Manor to complain, had paused to watch the Heir as he attempted a three-point turn in the JCB and jammed it across the ditch. One of them, a stranger to the area, looked into the bucket of the JCB.

'Been fishing?' he inquired, 'You've grubbed up something horrible.'

The Heir climbed up the side of the ditch to look. 'Did you mention a fish?'

'It must have come up with the water,' the stranger said.

United looked into the bucket. Thrashing about in the muddy yellow water was a thing that looked more like a fish than, say, a bicycle. It had scales. It also had long pointed teeth, and whiskers, and feet.

It was not, come to think of it, all that much like a fish.

'It's an eft, that's what it is,' said one of the locals.

'What's an eft?' the Heir said. He had never spent much time in Grimsditch-on-Slype himself and he did not understand many perfectly ordinary words such as eft.

'A newt,' the stranger said. 'An amphibian.'

'That's never a newt,' United said. The thing was opening and closing its mouth at him, as if miming unprintable words, swivelling its eyes and rippling its nasty whiskers. He reached into the bucket and seized it round the middle. It bit him.

'It's biting you,' the stranger said.

United raised the eft in his hand, and flung it far from him. It went end over end, through the air, and landed with a plop, somewhere out of sight.

'Gone into the river, I shouldn't wonder,' the stranger said.

'Now you're here,' said one of the locals, 'you might as well come up to the Manor with us. We're wanting a word with your old man.'

'If you're referring to my father, Lord Grimsditch, mind your manners,' the Heir said haughtily, 'but go and see him by all means. I have other fish to fry.'

'Other efts,' the stranger said with a meaningful smile and went off towards the bus stop, but the villagers, who were actually the Parish Council, went on up the hill to the Manor to complain to Lord Grimsditch about his son. They had an itemised bill for damages.

Soon afterwards Lord Grimsditch came storming down the hill waving the itemised bill in his gouty fingers.

'Wastrel,' he roared. 'Ne'er-do-well! You've not been home five minutes and you've gone through a water main, knocked down the war memorial and undermined the Co-op.'

'You told me it was time I got my hands dirty,' United complained.

'I didn't tell you to flatten the place in the process,' Lord Grimsditch bellowed. 'Go away! Go and make your fortune somewhere else. Go to America.'

'Why?' United asked.

'People do,' his father said. 'Usually they don't come back,' he added happily. 'Oh, take your JCB and go where you like. Just stay out of my road.'

The Heir got back into the driving seat, started the engine and executed a sixteen-point turn. Finally he got out of the ditch and growled towards the A1, and that, for ten years, was the last anyone saw of him, although there were the usual reports on the news that night: *Grimsditch Heir involved in punch-up at Heathrow.*

United Blackett went to the United States and made his fortune doing something he never talked about. Meanwhile, back in Grimsditch-on-Slype, things were happening. They were mostly things connected with water. Mains burst unexpectedly, drains were blocked, lavatories overflowed, and overnight the River Slype was emptied of fish. Then fishermen started to disappear as well.

One afternoon, in the middle of the High Street, a manhole cover shot up in the air on a jet of water and out of the manhole something began to emerge. It was long and pale and glistening, its pulpy body in segments so that it seemed to be made of soft white motor tyres. At one end there was a kind of a face with a gaping mouth full of sharp teeth and a fan of whiskers like antennae around its rubbery lips. The Chairman of the Parish Council, who happened to be crossing the street, recognised it at once.

'It's the eft,' he said. 'It's the eft young Blackett dug out of the Grimsditch.'

He started to say it to a passer-by but while he was speaking the creature leaned over in a casual manner and ate the passer-by: one gulp and a shiver all along the length of the motor tyres. Then it belched contentedly, hauled the rest of its considerable length out of the manhole and headed for the river, scooping up pedestrians as it went.

The Chairman of the Parish Council took off in the opposite direction towards Slype Manor. Lord Grimsditch was in the study, playing with his computer, but he leapt to attention when he heard what the Chairman of the Parish Council had to say.

'My son's at the bottom of this,' he groaned. 'My heir. I might have guessed.'

'I wouldn't say that,' the Chairman of the Parish Council said. 'He wasn't to know his eft was going to grow.'

'An eft?' Lord Grimsditch said. 'Does that sound like an eft to you?'

'It looked more like a worm to me,' the Chairman admitted, 'if you except the teeth, and the whiskers, and the swivelly eyes – and the feet.'

'Feet?'

'Only little feet – compared to the rest of it – but, yes, feet.'

Lord Grimsditch and the Chairman of the Parish Council went to the computer, logged on and looked up efts. It told them nothing about efts that they did not know already. Then they looked up worms. There was not a lot about worms, either.

'I don't know about you,' the Chairman of the Parish Council said, 'but when I was a lad we didn't have the Net. We had books.'

Although Lord Grimsditch called the room his study there were no books in it, just a computer. He walked down to the village with the Chairman of the Parish Council and they went to the public library to look up worms in a book. There they learned that a Great Worm is a particularly British species of dragon.

'Some of them are legless,' read the Chairman of the Parish Council. 'They don't have wings, they don't breathe fire – they emit toxic funes.'

'I thought you said it had feet,' said Lord Grimsditch.

'They're not much use to it overland, though,' the Chairman said. 'More like paddles. It goes upon its belly.'

'What does it eat? Dragons eat maidens. It's not after our maidens, I hope.'

'Just about anything,' the Chairman said. 'Sheep, cattle … I saw it down a traffic warden. And I think we can make an educated guess about where the fish went.'

'Where?' Lord Grimsditch said.

'Forget it,' the Chairman sighed. 'It's gone down to the river and it won't find anything to eat. Any day now it will come back out and start ravaging the country-side.'

'The Government will have to do something,' Lord Grimsditch said. 'This could be a national emergency.'

'The Government?' the Chairman said. 'The Government's in London. You load yon worm on to a flatbed truck and drive it down to Westminster and they might sit up and take notice. Otherwise we can sit here and whistle.'

He looked out of the window. It was

growing dark but a long pale shape was making its slimy way out of the river, head darting from side to side, tail switching. Every time it breathed out, a cloud of murky vapour rose from its mouth and birds dropped dead from the sky.

'That'll be the toxic fumes,' Lord Grimsditch said.

The Great Worm came to the Grimsditch, paused, hoovered up a sheep and oozed into the long broad dent where it seemed to settle and spread. It closed its wicked eyes and fell asleep, just where the Devil himself had fallen asleep all those centuries before.

The first anyone in London heard of the Great Worm of Grimsditch was when people turned up at Kings Cross Station to meet the 8.04 from Newcastle, due in at 11.16. Shortly after noon a message came through on the public address system. 'We would like to apologise for the late running of this service. This has been caused by a worm on the line.'

'Makes a change from leaves on the line,' people remarked, and sat back to wait.

But after a few weeks there were still delays due to a worm on the line. Word got around that this was no ordinary worm. ITN sent a television news crew to investigate. They were giggling a bit as they drove into Grimsditch-on-Slype and set up their camera outside the station.

'Where's this worm then?' said the interviewer to a man who had been waiting three days for a train.

The man pointed. 'See that hill?'

They looked. In the western sky the sun was setting behind a long pale ridge of what looked like ploughland.

'That's the Worm.'

'Where?'

'The hill. That's the Worm.'

'Pull the other one,' the cameraman said. 'I heard it came out of the sewers.'

'It's grown a bit,' the man said. 'It has a hearty appetite.'

At that moment the Worm raised its head, yawned and ingested a passing herd of cows.

'Strike a light,' the cameraman said.

The Worm breathed out. A dark cloud rose above it and obscured the setting sun.

A hang-glider plummeted.

'Wait till it brings down a 747,' the man said. 'Then we'll see some action.'

That night, on the news, the whole country saw the Worm. It was now so large that it was impossible to show all in one piece. The cameraman had to make a tracking shot from the car as the crew drove past it. The film ended sharpish as the Worm swallowed the car. Next day the papers were demanding Government intervention. Questions were asked in the House of Commons.

'What will happen,' said the Leader of the Opposition, 'if it decides to move south?'

'DRAT will take decisive action,' the Prime Minister said, decisively. DRAT was the Department of Rural Affairs and Transport. Bad politicians were sent there as a punishment.

The Secretary of State for DRAT was sent to Grimsditch-on-Slype on a fact-finding mission. People watching the ten o'clock news saw him standing on the edge of the Grimsditch looking at the Worm which was licking its rubbery lips.

In London the Prime Minister spoke to the nation.

'I have every confidence in my Right Honourable Friend. He is a man of integrity.'

An assistant whispered in his ear. 'Prime Minister, he has just been eaten.'

'He *was* a man of integrity.' The Prime Minister looked sober and sincere. 'He was a great public servant. Unfortunately he has become swallowed.'

In the morning he announced a programme of contiguous culling. 'The Worm will be cut into contiguous slices,' he said. 'The Army has been called in.'

'They don't know owt,' Lord Grimsditch sighed. He and the Chairman of the Parish Council were watching the news on television in the study at Slype Manor. According to the library book it was no use cutting Great Worms into slices. The pieces just grew back together again.

'Should we warn them?' the Chairman said. A convoy was coming up the A1 from Catterick.

'They'll find out soon enough,' Lord Grimsditch said.

Three battalions went down the Worm, followed by the usual snacks of cows, sheep, pigs and goats and the 6.25 from Edinburgh which was passing through Grimsditch-on-Slype as the Worm rolled down to the river to drink. The water level dropped dramatically.

'Dammit, man,' the Chairman said. 'We can't just sit here and watch.'

Lord Grimsditch appeared to have fallen asleep. The Chairman of the Parish Council tiptoed over to the computer and sent an email to the Heir at **www.grimsditcheir.com**.

United, come home. Your country needs you.

United mailed back: *I find that hard to believe. Twenty-nine different countries have decided that they don't need me.*

The Chairman of the Parish Council responded: *Haven't you heard about the Worm?*

Yes. Jolly hard luck. Nothing to do with me.

The Chairman flung himself at the keyboard. *Oh yes it is. That Worm is your eft. It went down into the sewers and grew.*

That's an urban myth.

Wrong. It's a rural fact. The fate of the nation is in your hands.

United had improved with age. He had grown a beard and a conscience. He logged on to **www.wisewoman.co.uk** where he knew he would find the answer to everything.

I wondered when you'd show up, the Wise Woman said.

You've got to help me.

No, I haven't.

I beg you.

That's a start.

The future of my country is in my hands. I have to slay the Worm.

Very well. Get yourself some decent armour and make a vow.

Any vow?

No, this vow. When the Worm is slain you'll sacrifice the first living thing you meet afterwards or the Grimsditches will be cursed for nine generations. Now give me your credit card details.

United returned to Grimsditch by night, driving the JCB that he had parked at Heathrow ten years earlier. People saw the nine-mile tailback on the A1. 'Ah, the Heir is back,' they said. It was almost dawn when he reached Slype Manor.

'What are you doing here?' his father said ungratefully, when he saw who was underneath the beard.

'I have come to slay the Worm!' United cried.

'Slay it? Have you seen it?' Lord Grimsditch said. 'It's longer than the Wetherby bypass.'

'I must slay it,' United said, 'or perish in the attempt. I have come to atone for my misspent youth.'

'That's fair enough,' said his father. 'It's all your fault, anyroad up.'

'But I have vowed a vow,' United said, 'to sacrifice the first living thing I see when I return. I'll blow three blasts on my horn to let you know the Worm is dead, but *don't come out to meet me* or I'll have to sacrifice you. Send the dog.'

There was something wrong with this suggestion but in the heat of the moment neither of them could think what it was.

When daylight came United went out and climbed into the only armour he had: the JCB that his father had given him, that he had been driving all those years ago on the day when he had dug up the fatal eft. He drove down to the Grimsditch and as it heard the menacing snarl of the diesel engine the Worm raised its fearsome head. Without hesitating United roared on, the mechanical digger flailing, the bucket swinging. He smote the Worm, he burrowed into it, he severed it, bits of worm flew hither and yon, and when the severed bits tried to grow back together he scooped them up in the bucket and flung them in the river.

The Worm fought back with its razor teeth and venomous whiskers, but United had known that he was entering a hard-hat area and his head was covered. A gas mask protected him from the toxic fumes and the reeking worm blood flowed harmlessly by. At last the frightful beast lay dead.

United blew three blasts on the horn of the JCB and went wearily up the hill to Slype Manor where Lord Grimsditch and the Chairman of the Parish Council were flinging open the doors to greet him.

'Get back, you silly old fool,' United yelled. 'Send out the dog!'

'What dog?' said the Chairman of the Parish Council. 'You haven't got a dog.'

United stood aghast as his father came closer, but almost as he reached him what  should come snaking round the corner but the tail-end of the Worm, writhing and thrashing and tying itself in knots, looking for another bit to join up with. United snatched off his hard hat, flung it down upon the last of the Worm and squashed it flat.

His mobile rang.

There was a text message from **wisewoman.co.uk**. *That was cheating. You were supposed to kill the first living thing you met. The Worm was technically dead.*

'You know what this means?' United said to his father. 'For nine generations, no Grimsditch will die in his bed.'

'So what's new?' Lord Grimsditch said, clapping him on the back. 'I was a Blackett before I was a Grimsditch. No Blackett ever died in his bed; we're builders.

'Blacketts die with their boots on, my boy. Let's go and celebrate.'

CORSICA

SARDINIA

ITALY

GREECE

SICILY

ARGOS △

Cave of
the Graeae

TUNISIA

CIRCU

The Gorgon
Medusa's
Island

LIBYA

△ The Kingdom of Acrisus and
   where the Medusa was born.

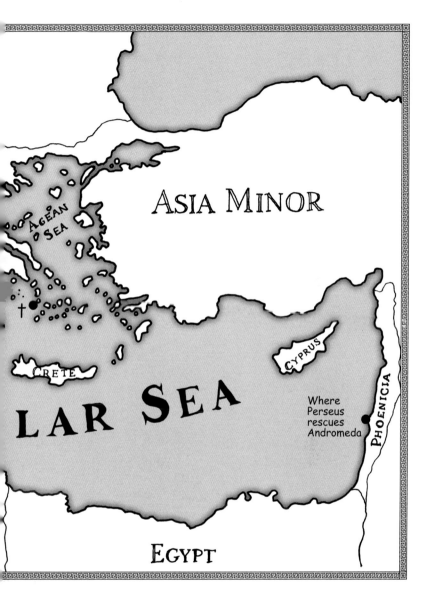

ASIA MINOR

AEGEAN SEA

CRETE

LAR SEA

CYPRUS

PHOENICIA

Where
Perseus
rescues
Andromeda

EGYPT

† Seriphos
Kingdom of Polydectes where
Danae and Perseus were washed
ashore.

Perseus the Hero

Retold by Geraldine McCaughrean

The first thing I remember is the sea –
being out at sea. There were waves all
around, and my mother was crying. I cried,
too, but only with cold and hunger. I was
too young to share my mother's horror and
sadness. I had still to learn how cruel
people can be.

My grandfather had cast us both adrift in a leaky old trunk meaning us to die. He was a deeply superstitious man, and when a fortune-teller predicted that his own grandson would kill him, he gave a terrible, shrill laugh and said, 'In that case I shall never *have* a grandchild!'

He locked his only daughter, Danae, in a tall tower, telling himself that a girl caged like a songbird, high up, was out of reach of men. Therefore, she could never give birth to a child. Turning the key in the lock, throwing the key into the sea, my grandfather must have finally felt free of fear.

A year later, I was born.

Grandfather was terrified. Too superstitious to murder us with his own hands, he decided to let the sea do it for him. So he bundled Mother and me into a leaky old chest and cast us adrift on the sea.

The sea (or the gods) must have loved us more than Grandfather. After three days, there came the crash of waves, a crunching judder and the trunk turned upside down. It spilled us out on to the soft, pale sand of an island, where we lay and dried in the sun. A noisy hubbub of voices! Then rough, brown hands were pulling us up the beach, out of the chilly surf, to safety and a new life. Finally my mother stopped crying.

Last month her tears began again. I could almost taste salt on my tongue and smell the inside of that leaky trunk. Such memories soak deep into a boy's soul.

In this new land to which the fishermen brought us, nobody had ever seen anyone as beautiful as my mother. The King himself stared at her, like a child staring at a tray of sweets. When he found out she was of royal blood, he made up his mind, then and there, to marry her.

At first he was patient. Every year, once a year, King Polydectes proposed to her. We used to laugh about it, Mother and I. I was not surprised he found her beautiful. She is. I was not surprised she turned down the King's offer. (He is smelly and rude and eats with his mouth open and picks his ears with a twig.) Suddenly, last month, the joke stopped being funny.

'Polydectes says this time he won't take no for an answer, Perseus!' cried Mother. 'He says he will marry me, whether I like it or not!'

'He will have to kill me first!' I vowed,

but for some reason that only made her sob harder than ever. I mounted guard at the door, and when the King's soldiers came to fetch her to the palace, I sent them home with bloody noses and bent swords.

Next time, King Polydectes sent for me rather than Mother. He did not look as angry as I had expected. 'All these years, Perseus, I have allowed you and your lovely mother to live in my country. I gave you a house. I sheltered you from your enemies. Don't you think that Danae owes me something in return?'

'If there is a debt, sir, I will gladly pay it,' said I. 'I am willing to serve you, but you must leave Mother alone!'

'Ah but what service could you *possibly* do me?' said Polydectes, and I, like a fool, fell straight into the trap.

'Name it!'

The King appeared to be thinking, his face sunk in his hands. Now I realise, he must have been trying not to laugh. When he looked up, there was a nasty glint in his eye. 'Fetch me the head of the Gorgon Medusa and we shall consider the debt repaid ... Oh but of course you will never dare such a dangerous feat.'

'Of course I will! I'll do it! Just wait and see! I shall come back within the month!' said I, and wondered why the King's laughter followed me out of the palace.

My only problem was that I had never heard of the Gorgon Medusa. Who was she? What was she? I did not know then that she had killed every hero or traveller who ever laid eyes on her. I did not know that her hair was a tangle of poisonous snakes, her face so hideous that it could snap a man's nerve like a pencil lead.

I did not even know how to *find* the Gorgon Medusa, because nobody who had found her lair had ever lived to say where it was.

'You must ask her sisters, the Graeae,' they told me. 'Only they have the information you need ...' And so I set off to find the Graeae.

After I had gone about a mile, I came across a shield. It was just lying in the middle of the road – a perfectly crafted disc of bronze. Its lining was as shiny as the silver sea. A useful find for a young man on a quest. But who could have left it there? You would almost have thought it had dropped out of Heaven. So I picked it up, gave thanks to the gods, and hurried on.

After another mile, I came across a helmet. It was just lying in the middle of the road – almost as if it had just dropped out of Heaven. A useful find for a boy in my situation. So I picked it up, gave thanks to the gods and put it on.

My feet disappeared – not just my feet, but my knees and hands and elbows! In fact wherever I looked for myself, I seemed to be missing. I had become invisible!

'Praise the gods for sending me such magic!' I said out loud and ran onwards, taking the helmet on and off, appearing and disappearing like a magician's rabbit.

After another mile, I came across a pair of sandals. They were just lying in the middle of the road, almost as if they had just dropped out of Heaven. A useful find for a boy with a long journey ahead of him. Perhaps, after all, that story of Mother's was true.

Every night of my childhood Danae told me the same unlikely story. I thought it was just a fairy tale to send me to sleep – bedtime make-believe, a fantasy. She told me how she had lived, week after week, shut up in that tall prison tower, with nothing but the stars and the birds for company. Half mad with loneliness, she had called and pleaded for her father to set her free – to let her see another human face – to let her hear a friendly voice. The tower had no door, and it rose almost as high as the moon. But someone heard her cries. Zeus, Father of the Gods, peeped in one night, through her tiny window, and liked what he saw. Not wanting Danae's beauty to go to waste, he turned himself into a shower of gold and trickled in at the window, like silk threading the eye of a needle. The gold dust settled on her eyes, on her hands, on her lap.

The words of Mother's story were always the same. *'You are the son of Zeus, my love, and the gods will always watch over you. Now go to sleep, my little hero, and dream of the gods.'*

'Thank you!' I shouted at the sky, then I bent and pulled on the sandals.

One step more and I was off the ground, another and I was walking on the wind.

'Praise to the gods!' I shouted. 'Flying *shoooooes*!' and away I flew, towards the red sunset, appearing and disappearing as I went.

I must have looked like a winking star.

The Graeae live in a cave: a grey home well suited to three grit-grey hags. They were quarrelling when I got there. I believe their life must be one long squabble.

'Give me the eye now, sister. It's my turn!' said one.

'No! I only just got it, didn't I, sister?' said another.

'I don't care who has it,' said the third sister. 'I'm hungry. Give me the tooth!' They were arguing over a single tooth and a single bloodshot eyeball. Angrily they slapped and clawed at each other.

'You fool! Now look what you've done! You've made me go and drop it!'

The eyeball rolled across the floor of the cave and stopped at my invisible feet. Not that I needed the Helmet of Invisibility. Without the eye the Graeae were all three blind. The three hags began to feel about for it. 'Be careful!'

'Don't tread on it with your big feet!'

'It must be here somewhere.'

'It is,' I said. 'I have it in my hand.'

'Who said that?' The Graeae sniffed at the air. They blundered towards me, upsetting the cauldron where their foul, grey dinner was stewing.

'Tell me where your sister Medusa lives and I shall give it back,' I said.

'Catch him! Kill him! Bite him!' cried the Graeae. 'Who has the tooth? Bite him for me!'

But I was too quick for them, dodging out of reach, juggling with the eye. 'Tell me where I can find the Gorgon Medusa.'

At last, cursing and grumbling, they gave in and told me: 'Sail six days towards the North Star, four days towards the eye of the Scorpion, two days towards the Little Bear, and you will see a bare rock set in the sea. Our sister lives there. *Now give us back our eye!*'

I was glad to be rid of it out of my hands. I tossed it in among them and was gone before their groping fingers could find it. But as I fled, I heard their hissing whispers behind me like a bagful of snakes: *'One sight of our sister and he'll be as dead as all the rest. No one can lay eyes on the Gorgon Medusa without his brain boiling and his soul melting and his heart breaking in two! She is just too vile!'*

Wearing the winged sandals, I had no need of a boat. I flew for three days towards the North Star, and all the while I wondered. For two days I flew towards the constellation of Scorpius and all the while I puzzled. For a whole day more I flew towards the constellation of the Little Bear, and all the while I was asking myself: how can you kill a monster without once laying eyes on it?

Far below, out of the silver wastes of water, jutted a jagged rock. Just at that moment, I caught sight of my face in the shiny lining of the shield – a worried face, a weary face – a face struck by a sudden, brilliant idea. If the gods had loaned me the helmet and the sandals to help me in my quest, then the shield too must have been given me for a reason. What if I was to use it like a mirror – to see the gorgon without truly *looking* at her?

I turned on my back, like a swimmer rolling over in the water. Holding the shield above me, I looked into its shining lining and saw there the reflection of the rocky island.

That is how I first caught sight of the Gorgon Medusa, hideous as Death.

Her body was a knobbly stalagmite. Her face was like a mosaic pavement rucked up and smashed apart by tree roots. Where hair should have grown on her head, a thousand serpents waved and wove and knotted.

At the sight of that hair, clammy sweat broke from my hands and armpits, and the snakes smelled it. The gorgon lifted up her face, scouring the sky, screeching in her own ear-splitting language. The sight was enough to freeze a boy's brain, to break his heart, to shiver his soul. But because I saw it all as a reflection, the full horror was blurred. It was like glimpsing a squid through choppy waves, like seeing a daubed painting of a horrible monster.

Pulling out my sword, never looking round, I flew lower – then lower still – until the hiss of that snaky hair was almost brushing my bare neck.

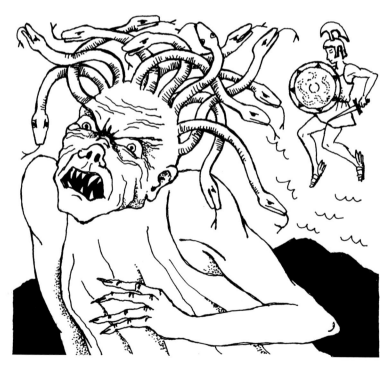

Her arms groped for me like the branches of a tree lashing in a gale. Her claws snagged the hem of my tunic and left it ragged. My head was full of her shrieking rage. The smell from her rotting prey made the air almost too thick to breathe. Her putrid breath clouded the metal of my shiny shield. Then I struck blindly over my shoulder – struck and struck again!

The gorgon screamed – a deafening mixture of rage and pain. I struck again – and something heavy fell with a thud on to the rock. The gorgon's head was off. And still I dared not look round to glory in my triumph. Suppose her eyes were still open? If I looked into those dead eyes, Medusa's ugliness might yet claim one last victim.

I had brought a sack along. It was an ordinary sack with no magic to it, but at least I was able to cram the severed head out of sight. I had to take it back with me, you see. Polydectes would want proof that the Gorgon Medusa was dead.

Suddenly I lost my balance. It was as if something had barged into me – something hard and warm like the flank of a horse. Could the gorgon still be living, then, even though her head was off? I looked into the shield and a searing white flash – sunlight probably – blinded me for a moment or two. I heard the ruffling of wings. Seagulls, I suppose, taking off in a flock from their grubby roost. When my eyes recovered, there was certainly a sprinkling of white feathers streaking the rocky shore.

As I flew over the desert regions of Greece, blood welled through the sack and dripped on to the sand below. And wherever those drops fell, snakes were born and wriggled away under stones or into cracks in the ground.

Flying over the coast of Phoenicia, I flew through the tale end of another story altogether ...

I looked down and saw a girl, dressed all in white, chained to a rock beside the sea. She was beautiful – almost as lovely as my mother. A massive shape was speeding towards her through the shallows – a darker green in the greenish sea. When it burst from the water, its head was all teeth and its colour was that of crocodiles and dragons, basilisks and snakes. Armoured with lizard scales, it had withstood axes and harpoons, tridents and swords as it stalked the coastal towns.

Nothing and no one had been able to stop it snatching its prey from fields and inn yards, and reaching in through the windows of houses ... Now it was all set to taste the sweetest morsel of all: the one meal it had wanted from the very start: the flesh of Princess Andromeda.

What was I to do? I had no extra-sharp weapons to pierce that leathery hide. Even if Zeus truly is my father, I have no superhuman powers to wrestle a beast like that. But I saw that girl's face when she caught her first sight of the sea monster. And that was enough to fetch me plunging out of the sky like a sparrowhawk.

I skidded through the sea's spray on my winged sandals, drawing my puny little sword. The blade snapped off instantly against the monster's snout. Coral-coloured teeth snagged in my collar and I was flung hard against the cliff. Helmet and shield and sandals fell into the sea. But as I lay on the shingle, winded and stunned, I found I still had hold of the sack.

So I pulled out the head and showed the monster something even more horrible than itself: the Gorgon Medusa's face.

At once the sea fell silent: no splashing, no thrashing, no spray. Andromeda still stood straining against the chains that bound her, but the monster in front of her moved not a muscle. There had been magic enough left in the mask of the gorgon to turn the creature to stone, there where it stood. The sea slopping against its granite flanks would never again wake that harmless, heartless mound of rock.

Having once seen Andromeda's lovely face, I would have married her whoever she was. It was a bonus to find she was a princess and that I was now son-in-law to a king.

'Stay,' said my new father-in-law. 'When I die, my throne will be yours.'

But I had another pressing appointment. I set sail the very next day with my new wife, and sailed without touching port, until we reached Seriphos, home of King Polydectes.

The streets were hung with scarves. The shrines were heaped with flowers. 'What is the celebration?' I asked a passer-by.

'The King's marriage, of course! The King is marrying that Greek beauty, Danae!'

Andromeda squeezed my hand. 'Didn't I tell you, Perseus? Sometimes beauty can be a woman's greatest curse.'

My eyes blurred over with anger. 'I know a curse stronger than that, my love,' I said.

I ran all the way to the temple, where Mother had taken refuge from that brute Polydectes. After weeks of siege, the King's soldiers had finally stormed the temple and taken Danae captive. Now she stood at the King's side, an unwilling bride at an unhappy wedding. The only guests were the ranks of soldiers making sure Danae did not escape.

'What of your promise, Polydectes?' I heard my voice boom through the temple. To my surprise, it was no longer a boy's voice. I must have gone away a boy and come home a man.

'Well?' said Polydectes with a smirk. 'I asked you to bring the gorgon's head and you failed.'

'Did I?'

'Clearly you were too much of a coward,' he sneered, 'or you would not be here now. Won't you congratulate your mother and wish us joy? I am sorry you missed the wedding.'

I did not lose my temper or reach for my broken sword. 'I will do better than that, Your Majesty,' I said. 'I shall give you a wedding present – *Mother, close your eyes!*'

Out of the sack I pulled the lifeless head of the Gorgon Medusa. Its snaky hair was lank and its toothy mouth was closed, but it still had horror enough to work its terrible magic.

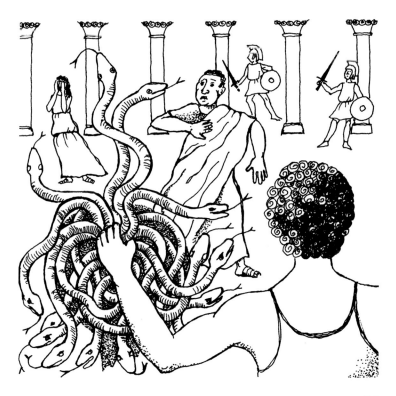

After I had put it away, I went and kissed Mother and she in turn blessed me for coming home. Meanwhile King Polydectes and his men made not a move. They looked on with staring eyes, frozen hands, half-drawn weapons, and did ... nothing. For the sight of the Medusa had turned them all to chalk-white stone.

Since Danae is now Queen, I, her son, am heir to the empty throne of Seriphos. I could stay here, or I could return with Andromeda to her father's kingdom. But first I have another place in mind: my grandfather's kingdom.

What? Do you think I want revenge for what he did to Mother and I? Not at all! To tell you the truth, I feel more pity than hatred for him. How can you hate a foolish, frightened, superstitious old man who has been scared half out of his wits by some lying fortune-teller? No, unlike Grandfather, I would never *think* of harming my flesh and blood. I ask you: do I look like a murderer?

* * * * *

On the far shore of the Circular Sea, near the crumbling ruins of a tall tower, the

Games have just begun. It is the festival of Apollo, and athletes from all over the mainland have come to compete for garlands of laurel. They race and wrestle. They throw the javelin and try to jump higher and farther than their rivals. The sun is hot, but a sharp wind off the sea dries their sweat in an instant and chills the old King who sits watching in the stands.

Tempted to show off his skill with a discus, young Perseus puts off the touching reunion. He puts off the moment when he will kneel in front of his grandfather and solemnly forgive the old man's unkindness. Instead, he enters the Games, and rubs chalk into his palms so as to grip the discus good and tight before letting it fly.

It is a good throw – by far the best of the day. The crowd gasp. A gust of wind catches the discus and blows it askew. It flashes into the crowd. There is a thud – just like the noise of the gorgon's head falling to the ground. A quite different noise runs through the crowd now – a groan of sorrow and shock and dismay. The discus has struck someone! The old King lies dead, his skull cracked open by a kilo of bronze.

No one holds Perseus to blame.

'A terrible accident,' they say.

'These things happen.'

'A man's death is ordained by the gods.'

'There is no dodging Fate.'

'And it was a *very* good throw.'

Medusa the Beauty

Retold by Geraldine McCaughrean

I was beautiful once – beautiful and young.
I was nothing like my triplet sisters, the
Graeae.

They were already old when they were
born. People stooped over their cradle to
admire their baby perfection and stepped
sharply back – *blurgch*!

There was that single, bloodshot eye for one thing. In time they learned to share it, but not out of love for one another. My sisters never even liked each other. Even after a year or two more, they had only managed to grow one tooth between the three of them. They had to learn to share that, too.

When they grew up from grisly children into grisly adults, and took themselves off to the middle of Nowhere, no one was sorry to see them go.

I was different. Everyone said so. 'How *different* Medusa is from her sisters – thank goodness,' people would say, gazing into my cradle. They meant that I was beautiful. Oh yes. Believe it, or believe it not, I was beautiful when I was young.

I was so lovely, in fact, that when I went walking down by the sea, the waves jostled for a glimpse of me. Those at the back heaved themselves up higher than those in front, until the sea grew rough and foamy. Inside each wave the fish gaped through their watery windows, and their mouths were bubble-round. '*Beauoootiful!*' they seemed to say.

The sea god Poseidon woke from sleep one morning, on the bed of Deep Ocean, and idly watched shoals of sardines and schools of dolphins all swimming in one direction overhead. He wondered where they were going, so he followed the glittering troupes of skipjack and eel, all the way from the Pillars of Hercules to the shores of the Circular Sea.

And there he saw ... well, he saw me. I was combing my long coppery hair and singing. Poseidon just stood there, waist-deep in the surf, staring. And I could do nothing but stare back at him. He was so – well, so godlike!

Suddenly his face took on a scowl. 'Huh! Another Andromeda, I suppose,' he said.

'I beg your pardon?'

The sea god's temper was making the sea quake and the skies darken overhead. His moods are as changeable as his watery realm – one moment calm and placid, the next stormy and wild. 'I know you mortals: vain and boasting.'

'I'm sorry?' I said, as rain began to slant between us.

'Over the sea, a king and queen have a daughter – a pretty child called Andromeda. But how that mother brags! On and on! 'My Andromeda is lovelier than all the stars in the sky! My Andromeda is lovelier than every blossom in the wood! My Andromeda is lovelier than any of Poseidon's mermaids! Huh! The arrogance of the woman! The insult!'

'Oh dear. She should not say such things,' I said. 'Beauty is a gift from the gods. It is no way to thank the gods – by insulting them!'

The rain slackened. The sea grew calm. Poseidon seemed soothed by my words. He came closer and began to study every detail of my face – the curls across my forehead, my lashes, my mouth. His fingers stroked my cheek. 'I will have to punish them, of course. They have to be taught a lesson,' he said.

'Sorry? Oh! Yes! Naturally. What are you going to do?'

'I think I shall send ...'

But then Poseidon seemed to change his

mind and stop. He did not tell me – he never told me – how exactly he had decided to punish the parents of Andromeda for their bragging. Perhaps he did not want me to think he was spiteful or bad tempered.

For a time we just talked. But after a while Poseidon began fooling about – splashing me and making me laugh. The more I laughed, the more he sighed. We were in love, of course, and the news did not take long to spread. Flocks of gulls carried it far and wide across the Circular Sea.

That is how Athena got to hear of it.

Athena, grey-eyed goddess of war, hates Poseidon. Ever since he sent a tidal wave washing through the white temples of her sacred city, Athens, they have been sworn enemies. Beneath her steel-grey breastplate, Athena's heart is colder than steel. She despises mortal women and she despises any god ready to squander his love on one.

And I *am* mortal. Unlike my ancient sisters whose old age will go on forever, Medusa will one day die. I think that in Poseidon's eyes that made me all the more appealing – like a spring flower, here and gone. To Athena, of course, it made me as unimportant as a worm.

And to spite her enemy Poseidon, Athena decided to spoil his happiness, to rob him of his pretty little mortal sweetheart.

I remember the day she came to visit me. She was so tall that she had to duck her head to come in through the door. She was so unsmiling that the figures on the tapestry behind me covered their faces with their hands. My heart shrank inside me.

'Foolish little mortal,' she said. 'How long do you suppose a mortal woman can keep the love of a god? Didn't you ever hear the saying: Beauty is only skin deep? Do you really suppose Poseidon will love you when you are old and grey?'

'I hope so. I know I shall still love him,' I said.

Athena carried a shield and on it the crest of a woman's head crowned with snaky hair. She carried a spear and, after brandishing it in my face, she struck me on the head so hard that I fell to the floor. Deep blackness swallowed me up. The last words I heard were Athena's: 'Well, no one will love you now, Medusa!'

The moment I awoke, I knew that I had changed. I put my hands to my face. It was puckered, like a purse pulled shut. My nose had been melted like a candle stub. My teeth leaned this way and that. My cheeks were hollow, my ears ragged. Worst of all was my hair. For where, before, glossy curls had tumbled down my back, now they lifted clear of my scalp, coiling and knotting of their own accord. Each strand was a snake, each snake a poisonous copperhead tasting the air with a forked, flickering tongue.

Deep in my brain, where the snakes were rooted, I sensed what the snakes were tasting. I could taste what they could taste. I even felt the stirrings of snaky thoughts: cunning and the desire to kill. I had become a gorgon.

I ran as far as the sea. There on the beach, standing with my hands in my hair, I screamed for Poseidon. *'Help me! Come and help me, my love!'*

He rose up out of the waves, but I saw his face flinch, his eyes turn away, revolted.

I knew I had changed, but until then I did not know how much. Only then did I discover just how ugly Athena had made me, inside and out.

I hated Poseidon then. I hated his fickle, shallow love that prized only the curve of a pretty leg, the shine in a pair of eyes. I hated him for proving Athena right: men care nothing about the woman *inside*, just the pretty wrapper she comes in.

From that day on I hated them all: blond, brown or black; young, old or middle-aged. I hated men for what they are, and women for having what I had lost. Athena did not just change the outside, you see: she managed to change the inside as well. Medusa the girl was gentle; Medusa the gorgon is full of venom and spleen.

Poseidon was immortal. He could look at me and all he felt was disgust. But whenever a mortal's eyes so much as glimpsed my ugliness, his soul smashed like a mirror. I quite literally frightened people to death.

For the safety of Mankind, Poseidon transported me to a rock far out at sea, away from the shipping lanes, away from the busy traffic of the seas. Still legends grew up of a hideous monster that could, with a single glance, shatter a man's soul like a lump of chalk. Those cobwebby crones the Graeae, squabbling over their single eye and their only tooth, cackled with spiteful joy at the thought of their pretty little sister losing her fabulous looks.

Nowadays, mothers tell their children, 'Behave yourselves! Eat your food! Tidy your room, or the Gorgon Medusa will come after you!' Superstitious sailors throw coins into the sea, saying, 'Oh Poseidon, do not wreck us with your storms! Don't let the winds carry us too near to the rock of the Gorgon Medusa!'

Kings send assassins to kill me, you know? The various kings of the various countries around the Circular Sea regularly send heroes to find out if I am real or just a grisly fairy tale. They send heroes to capture me, heroes to kill me.

They think they can creep up on me, my murderers. But I scent them long before they can even see me. Every strand of my hair, you see, is licking the smells off the air, day and night. Awake or sleeping, deep in my brain I smell trespassers even before they sail into sight. And then I turn to watch them coming closer and closer – those handsome young heroes, those brave warriors, those bold monster-slayers. I watch them sail ashore. I watch them climb out of their boats. I watch them look around for me, peeping through their fingers ... as if that will save them. Then their eyes meet mine, and that is the last sight they ever see.

The heroes never go home again. I see to that. I see to it with my yellow, reptile eyes, my scaly skin, my wriggling knot of hair. Over the years, their bones have piled up at my feet.

Don't blame me! Is it my fault that their hearts fail when they see me? Is it my fault that their kings go on sending them? Do you think anyone would *choose* to look as I look?

And it is not a sin, you know, to be ugly.

The gulls bring me news from every shore of the Circular Sea. It was they who told me more of the story of pretty Princess Andromeda. Apparently Poseidon 's punishment for her mother's bragging was to send a sea monster. Now it terrorises the whole kingdom, dragging itself out of the sea to snatch people out of the fields and houses. The only way to make it go away will be to sacrifice the lovely Andromeda; to feed her to the monster.

I wonder if her mother and father will be willing to pay such a price? I wonder if they would love Andromeda so much if she were not a *beauty*.

I hear from the gulls that my triplet sisters love me more these days, now that I am even uglier than they are. They refuse to tell anyone where I live, in case I should come to harm. I suppose that is a kind of love.

But they should not trouble themselves. I don't prize my life very much. It is not much of an existence, after all, standing here on this slimy rock, halfway between Nowhere and Nowhere Else; a prisoner of the sea. I would step off into deep water and drown myself ... but I must not die.

Inside me Poseidon's child is growing. What will it be like when it is born? Who will it take after: a god or a gorgon?

So I go on standing here, and while I do, I remember. I remember being beautiful. When the heroes leave me alone and there are no ships passing, I stand here with my eyes closed and pretend I am still beautiful. I remember how I looked in a mirror – lilac eyes, long lashes, curls across my forehead ... The memories still linger here, in one corner of this horrible head of mine.

What's that?

Suddenly my brain is full of scents. My hair is thrashing. And yet there is no ship! I can smell a man's sweat, sharp as lemons. But where is the man? Where? The sea around me is empty – a peaceful glitter of blue as far as the eye can see. Is someone swimming towards me? Is someone crawling towards me over the rocks? The air is full of his scent – an assassin's scent. *Show yourself, why don't you? I have not eaten yet today!*

The smell seems to be coming from above. I look up and see ... something too hideous to bear.

A circle of metal is hovering in the air, and in its bronze circle is the reflection of a woman. Where her hair should be, there are snakes. Where her nose should be, there is a stump like a burned down candle.

Is that *me*? Is that what I look like, then? No, no! No such face should exist!

Who has sent this mirror to taunt me with my own ugliness? I can feel the heart inside me struggling like an animal in a trap. It wants to break free. At the sight of that face, even *my* heart wants to break!

Come on, you invisible assassin – whoever you are – wherever you are! I can smell you! I know you are here! *Do your worst!*

There are feathers fluttering in my face. I can't see them but I can feel the breeze from them. I almost had him then! My hands snagged his clothing! Come on, whoever you are! I know what you've come for! Do your worst.

Do your best. Set Medusa free! For pity's sake.

* * * * *

A flash of light. A hiss of snakes. A scream cut short. And the Gorgon Medusa is dead. Her snaky head is gone, like the branches of a willow tree lopped off. Perseus, in his winged sandals and Helmet of Invisibility, has killed her.

But as she falls, the most amazing thing happens! Something escapes – as from a bottle whose cork has been removed. It is a flurry of white feathers. Medusa's child is seizing the chance to be born!

Two wings, a head, a mane ... the child of Medusa clearly looks nothing like its mother! A flank, four hooves, a plumy tail ... nothing like its sea-god father either.

The child of Medusa and Poseidon is a horse, as white as the sea's spray, more beautiful than any horse before it. And, unlike any other horse, Pegasus has wings. For a minute or two it stands on trembling, skinny legs on the barren rock. Then a large wave washes over the island. It sluices away the dead monster and the tangle of whitening bones. It washes over the little horse, like a blue hand stroking, and washes Pegasus clean of his mother's blood. Poseidon is blessing his son.

Wings dry, Pegasus takes to the air and rises towards the sky, whiter than the wheeling gulls, whiter even than the clouds.

Compared with Pegasus, the boy in his magic sandals is no more than a puny fledgling. Pegasus is a horse fit for the gods themselves to ride, and so he gallops up the sloping sky, through the foothills of sunset, towards the realm of the gods.

GLOSSARY OF NAMES IN PERSEUS THE HERO AND MEDUSA THE BEAUTY

ANDROMEDA (an-*drom*-uh-duh): The daughter of the King and Queen of Phoenicia. Poseidon, the god of the sea, sent a sea monster to ravage the countryside after hearing the Queen boast about her daughter's beauty.

APOLLO (a-*pol*-o): The god of light, music, poetry, dance, medicine and plague. He was the son of Zeus and Leto, and had a twin brother called Artemis.

ATHENA (a-*thee*-na): The daughter of Zeus, and goddess of wisdom, war, the arts and justice. There was much rivalry between Athena and Poseidon. She turned Medusa into a gorgon to get back at Poseidon.

CONSTELLATION OF SCORPIUS: A pattern of stars in the sky. Sailors used them to steer by.

CONSTELLATION OF THE LITTLE BEAR: A pattern of stars in the sky. Sailors used them to steer by.

DANAE (*dan*-ay-ee): The daughter of the King of Argos, and the mother of Perseus.

GORGON (*gor*-guhn): A monstrous creature with live snakes instead of hair. Anyone who looked at a gorgon was turned to stone.

GRAEAE (gree-ee): Medusa's three sisters, sharing one eye and one tooth. They told Perseus how to find the Gorgon Medusa.

HELMET OF INVISIBILITY or HELMET OF HADES (*hay*-deez): A helmet, given to Hades, god of the underworld, by the Cyclopes. It made whoever wore it invisible. Perseus wore it to defeat the Gorgon Medusa.

MEDUSA (muh-*dyoo*-suh): One of three gorgons in Greek mythology, and the only one who was mortal. She was turned into a gorgon by Athena.

PEGASUS (peg-a-sus): A winged horse. The offspring of Medusa and Poseidon.

PERSEUS (*per*-see-uhs): The son of Zeus and Danae.

PILLARS OF HERCULES *(hur-kyoo-leez)*: The pillars of rock on both sides of the Straits of Gibraltar. The pillars were once joined, but Hercules broke through the rock to create a gap to the ocean.

POLYDECTES (pol-i-*dek*-teez): The King of Seriphos, who sent Perseus on the quest for Medusa's head.

POSEIDON (puh-*sy*-duhn): The god of the sea and brother of Zeus and Hades. He was on bad terms with Athena. He fell in love with Medusa and was the father of Pegasus.

ZEUS (*zyoos*): The supreme ruler of Mount Olympus, where the gods lived. He was the father of Perseus.